The Wizard, the Fairy and the Magic

Helen Lester

illustrated by
Lynn Munsinger

M

PAN MACMILLAN CHILDREN'S BOOKS

Originally published in the United States of America 1983
by Houghton Mifflin Company.

Picturemac edition published 1993 by
PAN MACMILLAN CHILDREN'S BOOKS
A division of Pan Macmillan Limited
Cavaye Place, London SW10 9PG
Associated companies throughout the world

9 8 7 6 5 4 3 2

ISBN 0–333–57395–1

A CIP catalogue record for this book is available
from the British Library

Printed in Hong Kong

There once lived a Wizard, a Fairy, and a Magic Chicken.
Each thought, "I am the greatest in the world."
And each was very jealous of the other two.

"MY wand has a MOON on it," said the Wizard.

"MY wand has a STAR on it," said the Fairy.
"MY wand has a PICKLE on it,"
  said the Magic Chicken.

"I can kiss a pig

and turn it into a bicycle," said the Wizard.

"That's nothing," said the Fairy. "I can kiss a bicycle
and turn it into a bowl of soup."

"I can do better than that,"
  said the Magic Chicken.
"I can kiss a bowl of soup
  and turn it into a singing frog."

Each one always tried to outdo the others.

"I can make a hairy
monster with sharp teeth!"
bellowed the Wizard.

"I can make a bumpy monster with nine legs!"
screeched the Fairy.

"I can make a dotted monster with buggy eyes!"
yelled the Magic Chicken.

The monsters glared at the magicians and loudly said,
"GRRRRRROLPH!"

For the very first time the magicians agreed.

"RUN FOR YOUR LIVES!" they shouted.

"I will make a cloud to hide behind," gasped the Wizard,
  but that didn't stop the monsters.

"I will make thunder to scare them," puffed the Fairy,
but the monsters were not frightened.

"I will make lightning. That will make them go away,"
 cried the Magic Chicken, but they would not go away.
 Nothing worked.
"We'd better . . ." said the Wizard.
". . . try something . . ." said the Fairy.
". . . together!" said the Magic Chicken.

So they chanted, "One, two, three, GO!"
The cloud and the thunder and the lightning came together.
Suddenly it rained.

It rained so hard and the monsters got so wet that they shrank
until they were only very little monsters and
not scary at all.

"We did it!" cheered the Wizard, the Fairy, and the Magic Chicken.

"I must say, though," said the Wizard, "my cloud made the rain."

"Well," said the Fairy, "it was because of my thunder."

"But not without my lightning," said the Magic Chicken.

There once lived a Wizard, a Fairy, and a Magic Chicken.
They argued a lot,
but deep down they were very good friends.